For Olivia MW

SOUTHWOOD BOOKS LIMITED
4 Southwood Lawn Road
London N6 5SF

First published in Australia in 2000 by ABC Books for the
AUSTRALIAN BROADCASTING CORPORATION
GPO Box 9994 Sydney NSW 2001

This edition produced for The Book People Ltd.,
Hall Wood Avenue, Haydock,
St Helens WA11 9UL

Copyright © text Margaret Wild 2000
Copyright © illustrations Kerry Argent 2000

ISBN 1 903207 51 7

A CIP catalogue record for this book is available from the British Library.

The illustrations were painted with watercolour.
Set in Venetian
Designed and typeset by Monkeyfish
Colour separations by Modern Age, Hong Kong
Printed in Singapore by Tien Wah Press

2   4   5   3   1

Night Night!

MARGARET WILD & KERRY ARGENT

TED SMART

One evening as the sun was going down, the baby animals played and played and wouldn't stop playing. So Mother Sheep, Father Duck, Mother Hen and Father Pig called, 'Come on, everyone — off to your beds now, little ones!'

'Night night, my lovely lambs,'
said Mother Sheep, as she went
to tuck her little ones in.

'Cheep! Cheep! Tricked you!'
said the chicks.

'You cheeky rascals!
You're not my
lovely lambs!'
said Mother Sheep.

'Sweet dreams, my darling ducklings,'
said Father Duck, as he went
to tuck his little ones in.

'Oink! Oink! Surprise!'
said the piglets.

'You little scallywags!
You're not my darling ducklings!'
said Father Duck.

'Good night, my chicky chicks,'
said Mother Hen, as she went
to tuck her little ones in.

'Baa! Baa! Boo!' said the lambs.
'You naughty scamps!
You're not my chicky chicks!'
said Mother Hen.

'Sleep tight, my precious piglets,'
said Father Pig, as he went
to tuck his little ones in.

'Quack! Quack! Fooled you!'
said the ducklings.

'You fluffy tricksters!
You're not my
precious piglets!'
said Father Pig.

'You cheeky rascals!'

'You little scallywags!'

'You naughty scamps!'

'You fluffy tricksters!'

'Off to your beds now, everyone!'

'Night night, my lovely lambs,'

said Mother Sheep with a loving baa baa.

'Not yet!' said the lambs.
'Tell us one more story, please!'

'Sweet dreams, my darling ducklings,'

said Father Duck with a fond quack quack.

'Not yet!' said the ducklings.
'We want ten kisses each!'

'Good night, my chicky chicks,'

said Mother Hen with a gentle cluck cluck.

'Not yet!' said the chicks. 'We're thirsty!'

'Good night, my precious piglets,'

said Father Pig with a tender oink oink.

'Not yet!' said the piglets.
'We have to wee,

wee,

wee!'

'No more tricks now.'
'Settle down.'
'Snuggle up.'
'Sleep tight.'
'Night night!'